A Queen Named Esther

*"It's possible that you became
queen for a time just like this."*
—Esther 4:14

Bible A Queen Named Esther

© 2013 by Zondervan
ons © 2013 by Zondervan

ests for information should be addressed to:

ɪderkidz, 5300 Patterson Ave SE, Grand Rapids, Michigan 49530

ϽBN 978-0-310-74080-3

Zonderkidz is a trademark of Zondervan.

Editor: Mary Hassinger
Cover & Interior Design: Cindy Davis

Printed in China

ZONDERVAN.com/
AUTHORTRACKER
follow your favorite authors

ZONDERkidz

13 14 15 16 17 18 /DSC/ 12 11 10 9 8 7 6 5 4 3 2 1

Long, long ago, in a kingdom named Persia, there was a king that needed a new queen.

His helpers said, "King Xerxes, let us help you find
the perfect girl to be your queen."
King Xerxes thought about it. "Yes, find me the perfect queen."

The king's helpers found a girl named Esther. She was Jewish. Esther lived with her cousin, Mordecai. The men wanted Esther to meet the king.

Mordecai said to her, "Go and meet the king. It is a good idea."

So Esther met the king.
King Xerxes said, "You will be a very good queen."
And soon, she became Queen Esther!

Now, the king had many people helping him. Haman was the king's main helper. He was not a nice man. He hated Jewish people. Haman wanted them to go away. So he talked King Xerxes into making a new law. This law put all the Jewish people in danger.

Mordecai heard about the new law. He had to tell Esther!
Maybe she could help the Jews since she was now the queen.

"Esther!" Mordecai said. "God made you queen for a good reason. You must help save God's people from Haman's evil plan. Please talk to the king. Only he can save us."

Esther knew she had to help. It would not be easy. But she thought of a plan.

"Please help me be strong and brave, God," Esther prayed. "I need to go talk with the king."

"King Xerxes, may I ask you something?" Esther said.

"Yes," said the king. "Please ask me for anything. I will try to give it to you."

Esther said, "I am making a nice dinner. I would like you and your helper Haman to join me."

The king said yes.

So King Xerxes and Haman went to eat dinner with Queen Esther. They were very happy. The food was delicious.

The king asked Esther, "Now, Esther, what can I do for you?"

Esther said, "Haman tricked you! You signed a law. It says to get rid of all the Jews. King Xerxes, I am a Jew too!"

Haman could not believe his ears. Esther knew about his plan.
Now he would not get his way. The Jews would be safe.

King Xerxes was very angry. He could not believe his helper, Haman, would do this evil thing. He did not like being tricked!

The king called his guards.

He said, "Get Haman. Arrest him now."

The guards took Haman away. He would not be able to hurt the Jews ever again.

Now the king needed a new helper. He knew Queen Esther's cousin, Mordecai, was a good man. He asked Mordecai to be his helper now. Mordecai said, "Yes!"

The king was happy. He knew Esther and Mordecai were good people to have as helpers in his kingdom.

Esther and Mordecai were happy. They were glad they could help the king and God's people.

God's people were very happy too. Esther was a hero. She had saved the Jews from Haman's plan. They were all safe. "Hooray for Queen Esther!" they cheered.

God used Esther to save his people. Thank you, God!